Dino-Baby

Mark Sperring

illustrated by Sam Lloyd

BLOOMSBURY

NEW YORK   LONDON   NEW DELHI   SYDNEY

Do you remember when Dino-Mommy had a belly bump?

How you placed your head against it
and you heard a little thump?

And can you still remember all the things we said we'd do,
to help our dino-baby be a happy baby-boo?

We said...

Be quiet in the morning,
when you first get up...

because

thuds,

bangs,

and

crashes

will wake our dino-pup.

Don't play rough and tumble
with a little thing like this.

Instead be soft and gentle...

we all LOVE a dino kiss.

MWAAAH!

Don't snatch things away.

And always try to share.

Because when we play together...

it's much more fun and fair.

Toot! Toot!

Teach our dino-baby all the grown-up things you know...

like saying

please

and

thank you.

And all the best
places to go.

Whoops!

Show him how to **roar**

and **romp,**

to clomp

and stomp

and pound.

But when it's time for beddy-byes,
say, "Shhhh! Don't make a sound."

And over time, yes, day by day,
he'll grow up more and more.

9 feet

6 feet

3 feet

Until our little
dino-baby...

is a great BIG dinosaur!

For Mandy —M. S.

For Blake and Mae —S. L.

First published in Great Britain in May 2013 by Bloomsbury Publishing Plc
Published in the United States of America in October 2013
by Bloomsbury Children's Books
www.bloomsbury.com

For information about permission to reproduce selections from this book, write to
Permissions, Bloomsbury Children's Books, 1385 Broadway, New York, New York 10018
Bloomsbury books may be purchased for business or promotional use. For information on bulk purchases please
contact Macmillan Corporate and Premium Sales Department at specialmarkets@macmillan.com

Library of Congress Cataloging-in-Publication data
Sperring, Mark.
Dino-baby / by Mark Sperring ; illustrated by Sam Lloyd. — 1st U.S. edition.
pages   cm
Summary: When a new dino-pup arrives, big sister is reminded of some important things,
from being quiet in the morning to playing with him gently.
ISBN 978-1-61963-151-9 (hardcover) • ISBN 978-1-61963-152-6 (reinforced)
[1. Babies—Fiction. 2. Brothers and sisters—Fiction. 3. Dinosaurs—Fiction.] I. Lloyd, Sam, illustrator. II. Title.
PZ.S748985Din 2013   [E]—dc23   2013002688

Illustrations drawn with ink and digitally colored.
Typeset in Agent C
Book design by Zoe Waring

Printed in China by C&C Offset Printing Co., Ltd., Shenzhen, Guangdong
1 3 5 7 9 10 8 6 4 2 (hardcover)
1 3 5 7 9 10 8 6 4 2 (reinforced)